USBORNE BEGINNER'S KNOWLEDGE

SHIPS, SAILORS AND THE SEA

Caroline Young and John C. Miles

Designed by Mike Pringle

Illustrated by Colin King

Series Editor: Heather Amery
Consultant: John Robinson, Curator,
Science Museum, London

Contents

About this book

People have travelled on water for thousands of years. They have used boats to explore, find new lands, trade and to fight battles. This book tells you about the different ships people have built over the centuries, and how they sailed them.

Many different ships

Here are some of the boats and ships in this book, from the very old to modern ones.

paddle steamer

hovercraft

skin boat

Viking longship

submarine

Why does a boat float?

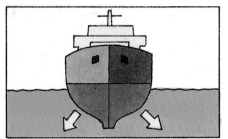

When a boat sits in the water, it pushes, or displaces, the water. The heavier the boat, the more water it displaces.

The displaced water pushes back against the outside of the boat with a force called upthrust.

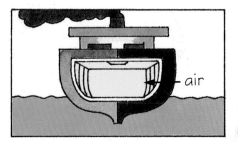
air

Because a boat is hollow, its downward push is not too strong for the water's upthrust to keep it afloat.

cargo

When cargo is loaded into a ship, it floats lower in the water. A ship must not be overloaded or it will sink.

A full load

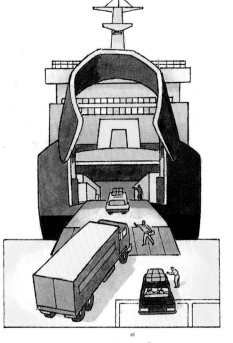

Ships can carry a great deal of cargo without sinking. This ferry can carry up to 100 heavy trucks or 650 cars on every crossing.

ocean liner

man o'war

yacht

tug

hydrofoil

log boat

kayak

Greek galley

Shaped for speed

hull

This speed boat has a slim hull which cuts through waves. It is so light that it almost skims over the waves.

Boatbuilders make the hull of a ship very smooth so that it will slide easily through the water.

This cargo ship is not built to go very fast. It has a wide hull so that it can carry a lot of cargo.

How do they move?

At first, people pushed boats along with their hands. Later, they made paddles and oars out of wood.

The wind has driven ships forward for thousands of years. It fills their sails and pushes them along.

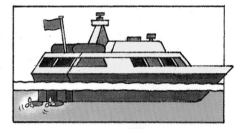

Engines were first fitted to ships over 200 years ago. They turned propellers, which moved the boat.

Crossing water

Thousands of years ago, there were no boats. People found crossing wide, deep stretches of water difficult and dangerous.

Although they could probably swim, there were some good hunting grounds they still could not reach.

Logs and skins

They saw that logs and reeds floated in water and they made them into the first boats.

animal skins

log raft

floating log

People sat on floating logs and paddled them along with their hands and feet. They could now cross water.

People also sewed animal skins together and filled them with air like a balloon. These floats carried them along.

Men tied several logs together with strips of skin to make a raft. It carried things as well as people.

Log canoes

The first boats were built over 12,000 years ago. Men used pointed stones or flints and animal horns to hollow out a log. To make the work easier, they lit a fire on the log to burn out the center.

Some log canoes were very large. One has been found that was big enough to carry 25 people. People used canoes to explore rivers and lakes and to fish.

Skin boats

People made skin boats by tying thin pieces of wood together to make a frame like a basket. They then stretched animal skins over the frame.

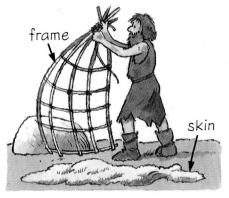

frame

skin

The skins were covered with tar to make them waterproof.

Paddles and oars

Later, people made paddles and oars to push their boats along faster. They helped them steer in the water.

Rowing with an oar was easier than paddling. Each oar was held in place by a loop on the boat's side.

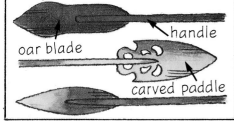

The first sails

Rowing or paddling long distances was tiring. Men saw that the wind could be used to blow their boats forwards.

They caught the wind in sails and this pushed the boat. The first sails were made of leaves or animal skins.

Reed boats

In some parts of the world, reeds grew by the banks of rivers and lakes. People made them into boats.

Steering oars to guide the boat.

Reeds drying.

Reeds being cut and stripped.

The reeds were cut and their leaves stripped off. They were then laid out in the sun to dry. The boatbuilders tied the dry reeds into bundles. These were then tightly tied together with ropes and shaped into a reed boat.

5

Ships of Ancient Egypt

The Egyptians were building boats over 5,000 years ago. They used them on the River Nile for trade, for fishing and to move their armies.

The first Egyptian boats were made of papyrus reed which grew by the banks of the Nile. Later, cedar wood was brought from Lebanon.

mast

sailor using lead line

thick rope

bow

The front of a ship is called the bow.

Thick rope pulled tight stopped the boat sagging at each end.

A trading ship had about 30 oarsmen.

Daring sailors

The Egyptians traded with countries all over the Mediterranean and the Red Sea. Their kings, called Pharaohs, sent ships to find gold and valuable timber. Egypt traded in grain, papyrus reeds and cloth with other countries.

Special expeditions set off for the Land of Punt, in East Africa, to bring treasures back to Egypt. The Pharaohs had beautiful jewelry made out of the precious stones, gold and ivory brought back from these trading trips.

This rock carving is about 5,000 years old. It shows Egyptian sailors loading a ship before a trading voyage.

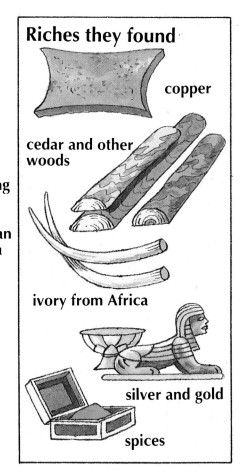

Riches they found

copper

cedar and other woods

ivory from Africa

silver and gold

spices

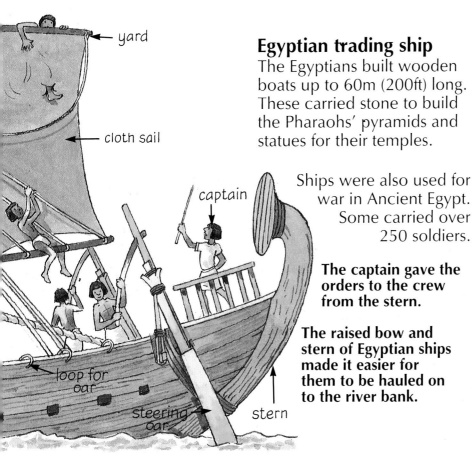

yard

cloth sail

captain

loop for oar

steering oar

stern

Egyptian trading ship

The Egyptians built wooden boats up to 60m (200ft) long. These carried stone to build the Pharaohs' pyramids and statues for their temples.

Ships were also used for war in Ancient Egypt. Some carried over 250 soldiers.

The captain gave the orders to the crew from the stern.

The raised bow and stern of Egyptian ships made it easier for them to be hauled on to the river bank.

Ropes made of twisted reed hold the sail and mast in place.

The rear of a ship is called the stern.

The lead line

Egyptian sailors needed to know how deep the water was so that they did not run aground on sandbanks.

rope

lead

A sailor dropped a lead weight over the side of the ship. When he pulled it up, the wet mark on the rope told him the depth of the water.

The Phoenicians

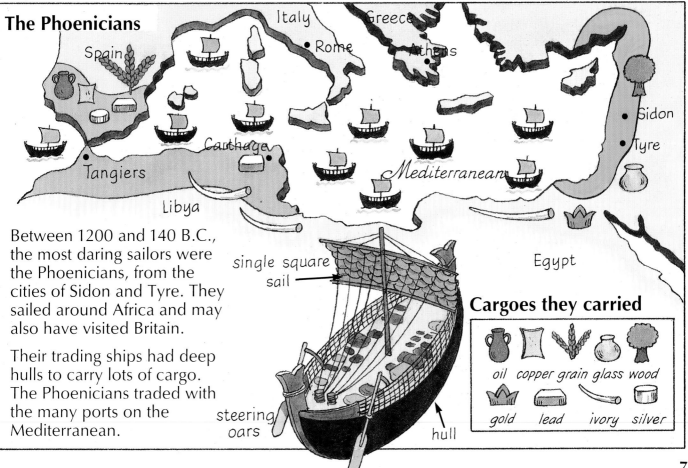

Italy
Greece
Spain
Rome
Athens
Sidon
Tyre
Carthage
Tangiers
Mediterranean
Libya
Egypt

single square sail

steering oars

hull

Between 1200 and 140 B.C., the most daring sailors were the Phoenicians, from the cities of Sidon and Tyre. They sailed around Africa and may also have visited Britain.

Their trading ships had deep hulls to carry lots of cargo. The Phoenicians traded with the many ports on the Mediterranean.

Cargoes they carried

oil copper grain glass wood

gold lead ivory silver

Ships of Greece and Rome

In Ancient Greece and Rome there were two main types of ship. One was for fighting battles and the other was for carrying cargo.

A Greek war galley

Greek galleys were up to 40m (131ft) long but were very narrow. A trireme in the 6th century B.C. had 170 oarsmen beneath the deck.

A Greek galley painted on an ancient vase.

Water and wine

The Greeks carried wine and water on board the galleys in pots called amphorae. Hundreds of amphorae have been found near wrecks of galleys.

Life on a galley

Life on a galley was very cramped. A trireme had a crew of 200 and many soldiers on board for a battle.

Greek ships were called galleys. They sailed to the Arctic Circle and southern

Britain as long ago as 300 B.C. They used landmarks, such as high hills to find the way.

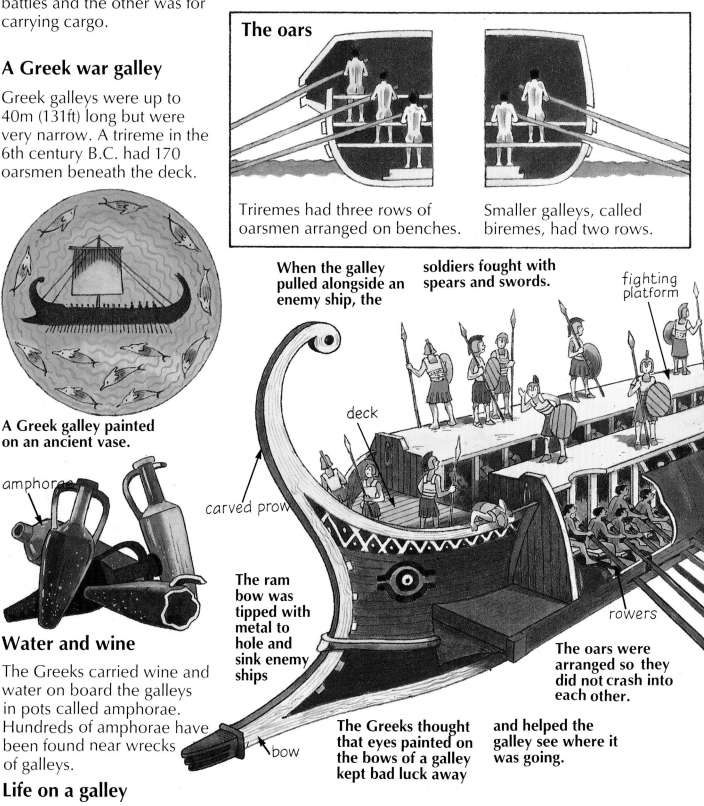

The oars

Triremes had three rows of oarsmen arranged on benches.

Smaller galleys, called biremes, had two rows.

When the galley pulled alongside an enemy ship, the soldiers fought with spears and swords.

fighting platform

deck

carved prow

The ram bow was tipped with metal to hole and sink enemy ships

rowers

The oars were arranged so they did not crash into each other.

The Greeks thought that eyes painted on the bows of a galley kept bad luck away

and helped the galley see where it was going.

bow

amphorae

There was no kitchen or toilet. At mealtimes, the galley was hauled ashore and food cooked on the beach.

The oars were about 4m (13ft)long and very heavy. The oarsmen rowed in time to tunes played on a flute.

Galley sheds

The Greeks used pine wood to build their galleys. It was light and made the ships easy to row, but could rot quickly in water.

Galleys were hauled out of the water when not in use.

They were kept in long sheds so that they would not rot.

Remains of galley garages have been found in Greece.

The mast and sail were taken down and left on shore before the battle. This left the fighting platform clear for soldiers.

helmsman

animal skins

oar

The sides of the galley were covered with animal skins to protect the oarsmen during battle.

The biggest ships

In the first century B.C., the Romans built even bigger ships to carry cargo. Some ships had four separate holds for grain. They were sometimes more than 50m (164ft) long and carried many tons of cargo.

Roman ships

The Romans built large merchant ships to carry goods to Rome from all over their Empire. They conquered lands all round the Mediterranean, North Africa and Northern Europe.

The Ancient Romans also used galleys in battles against the enemies of their Empire. Some Roman galleys had five rows of oarsmen. They were called quinqueremes.

The frames of Roman galleys were made of heavy oak and the hull of pine or cypress.

Roman ships often had a carved swan's head at the stern.

Smaller sail to help steer the galley.

steering oar

The Romans shipped cargo to Ostia, a port about 25km (16miles) from Rome. They brought wild animals back from Africa to fight their gladiators and carried rich cargoes of spices, gems and silk from Asia.

Viking seafarers

The Vikings lived in Scandinavia over a thousand years ago. They built fast, sturdy ships and were excellent sailors.

Life in a Viking settlement was hard. The Vikings built their longships to search for better farmland.

In about A.D. 795, the Vikings began to raid countries in Northern Europe. They seized land and stole many riches.

Viking longship

During the summer, the Vikings went raiding in longships. They could be rowed or sailed. This is a longship of about A.D.900.

Mast step

mast

The mast step was a large block of wood, fixed to the bottom of the ship. The mast fitted into it. A longship mast could be lowered or raised by ropes which helped to hold it upright when sailing.

Oars

A Viking longship usually had 16 oars on each side but some had as many as 30.

Steering oar

lever

A longship was steered with a single steering oar attached to a wooden block on the right of the ship. Worked by a lever, it made the ship turn to the right or left.

tar

steering oar

Where the Vikings went

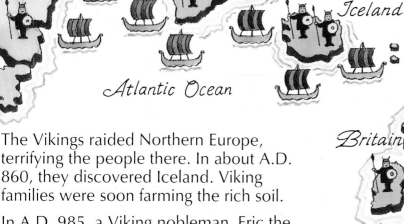

The Vikings raided Northern Europe, terrifying the people there. In about A.D. 860, they discovered Iceland. Viking families were soon farming the rich soil.

In A.D. 985, a Viking nobleman, Eric the Red, discovered Greenland. In A.D. 1000, Eric's son, Leif, landed in North America.

Sails

Early longship sails were made of lightweight cloth. Strips of leather strengthened them.

Wooden discs over the oar-holes kept water out when the longship was sailing.

Longships were about 24m(78ft) long and 5m(16ft) wide. They had enough room for up to 40 men on board.

The Vikings also built merchant ships. These only had oars at the bow and stern. They were wider than longships to carry more cargo.

Port and starboard

The Viking steering oar was always on the right side of the ship. This side became known as the steerboard, and later, starboard side.

Because a ship with a steering oar was always tied up to a dock on its left side, the left side of a ship became known as the port side.

Carved bow

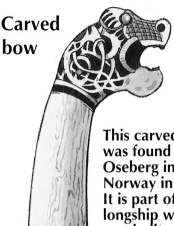

This carved bow was found in Oseberg in Norway in 1904. It is part of a longship which was built over a thousand years ago.

Viking boatbuilders carved the bows of their ships into shapes such as dragons and other fantastic beasts.

Shipbuilding

Vikings made clinker built ships. This means that the planks that made up the sides of the boat were overlapped.

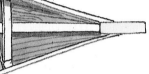

The planks were fixed together by long iron nails. The boatbuilder plugged the gaps between the planks with animal hair dipped in tar to make them watertight.

After the hull was built, large curved pieces of wood were fitted into it and tied into place. This inner frame made the hull stronger.

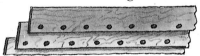

11

Sailors of the Pacific

For hundreds of years, the most skilful seafarers lived around the Pacific Ocean. They sailed many thousands of miles and invented the compass and the map.

The Chinese built three-masted ships hundreds of years before Europeans.

sails of matted reed

wooden poles to stiffen sails

Chinese sailors invented special watertight compartments for cargo.

Chinese junk

This is a Chinese ship of about a thousand years ago, called a junk. It has a flat bottom to carry more cargo.

high stern

The rudder

Chinese shipbuilders probably invented the rudder.

rudder

About 1,000 years ago, rudders were fixed to the stern of junks. They steered a ship more accurately than steering oars.

The voyages they made

The Chinese sailed all over the East in the 1400s. They traded silks and spices and made maps of the routes.

China

Arabia

India

Pacific Ocean

Africa

The Chinese traded with Africa, India and Arabia. They were often out of sight of land so could not use landmarks to guide them.

Chinese sailors made the first compass over 800 years ago. It was probably a magnetized needle, which pointed north in a bowl of water.

How they found their way

needle

Compasses like this one were used in China until the 19th century.

European compasses were mounted on a card with directions written on it.

Pacific islands

People sailed to the Pacific Islands hundreds of years ago, and settled there. They may have come all the way from Egypt or India in their small boats.

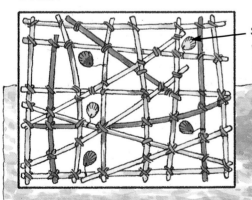

shells were islands

The islanders were excellent sailors and navigators. They made maps to show islands, winds and ocean currents out of sticks and shells, like the one in this picture.

Pacific sailors also found their way by noting the position of the sun and stars.

They knew that clouds formed over land and that birds flew between islands.

A Polynesian boat

The small boat-shaped float keeps the canoe stable. It is called an outrigger.

Some log canoes were up to 30m(100ft) long and had a cabin between the boat and the outrigger.

bamboo mast

outrigger

The Polynesian Islands are in the south Pacific. Polynesian sailors sailed hundreds of miles in small wooden boats. The main part of the boat is a hollowed-out tree trunk.

Fishbone, coral and stone were the boat-builders' tools. A smaller, hollowed-out float was often attached to the canoe with ropes and wooden poles.

Ships of the Middle Ages

Until the end of the 11th century, people built ships just as the Vikings had done. They had a single square sail and oars.

Ships on seals

Medieval towns had their own official seals. They were used to seal documents with the mark of the town.

This is the seal of the port of Winchelsea, England.

Towns which were also ports often had a ship on their seals, like this one.

A sea voyage

People wanting to travel by ship went to the harbor and made a contract with a captain. Ships could only sail when the wind was right.

This is a picture from the Bayeux Tapestry. It shows William the Conqueror invading Britain in 1066.

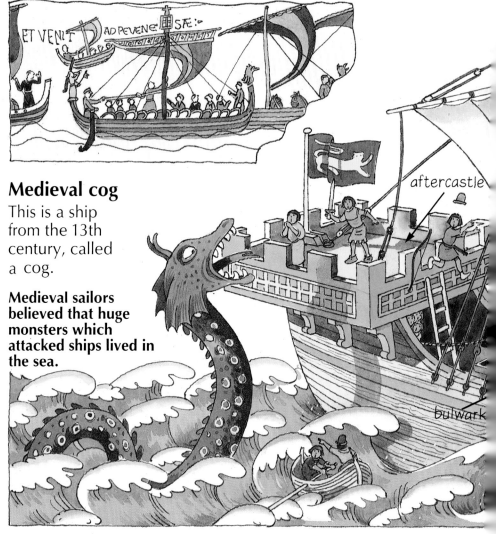

Medieval cog

This is a ship from the 13th century, called a cog.

Medieval sailors believed that huge monsters which attacked ships lived in the sea.

aftercastle

bulwark

Passengers travelled on deck with a space only 2m (6ft) by 0.6m (2ft) to sleep in.

Fruit and vegetables went bad, and there was only dried or salted food and stale water. Passengers often fell ill.

look-out post
or crow's nest

yard

Fighting castles

During the 13th and 14th centuries ships were fitted with fighting platforms at each end. They were called forecastles and aftercastles.

At first, the castles were taken down after battle. Later they became a permanent part of a ship. The spaces underneath them became cabins.

forecastle bowsprit

archer

anchor

Venice

Venice, in north-eastern Italy, was a rich city state in the 14th and 15th centuries. It was a centre for shipping and trade.

Silks, spices, jewels and gold were brought overland to the Mediterranean coast and shipped to Venice by galley. The city ruled these trading routes for over 200 years.

Venetian ships had two or three sails and up to 150 oarsmen. They sailed to India and to Northern Europe.

Galley slaves

Being at sea for months was boring. A game of dominoes or dice passed some of the uncomfortable days away.

Some European sailing ships had oars as well as a sail until the 16th century. Galley slaves were often criminals who were sent to work the galleys instead of being put in jail.

The galley slaves rowed in hot, cramped conditions. There were no toilets and rats and fleas were common. They were fed the poorest food and had to sleep at their oars. Many slaves died at sea.

Route to the East

About 500 years ago, Europeans began looking for a quicker route to the East. Control of this trade route would lead to great wealth. Two famous explorers who longed to find it were Christopher Columbus and Vasco da Gama.

The overland route

Goods from the East had to be brought overland by camel to ports on the Mediterranean. This was a journey of over 10,000km (6,250 miles). They were then shipped to Europe.

Bartholemew Diaz

In 1488, the Portuguese sailor Bartholemew Diaz sailed as far as the Indian Ocean. He turned back without realizing that he had almost reached the East.

Columbus' ships

Columbus' ships were called the *Santa Maria*, the *Nina* and the *Pinta*. The *Santa Maria* probably had five sails and a crew of about 40 men.

Caravels

The *Nina* and the *Pinta* were smaller, and had been trading ships called caravels before Columbus' voyage. They were only about 16m(55ft) long.

Christopher Columbus

Christopher Columbus was born in Genoa, Italy, in about 1451. He was sure that a sea route to the East existed, and he was determined to find it.

Columbus thought that if he sailed westwards across the Atlantic from Europe for about 4,000km (2,500 miles), he would reach Asia.

He spent many years trying to get money to prove his theory. Finally, in 1492, Queen Isabella of Spain gave him money and three ships.

lateen sails

These lateen sails are triangular and slant downwards.

Columbus' first voyage

Columbus left Palos in southern Spain in August, 1492. He bought some gifts on the Canary Islands for the Great Khan of China.

He soon realized that the Atlantic was wider than he had thought. After nine weeks, land was sighted. It was the Bahamas.

He was so sure that he had landed in China that he set sail to find Japan. Instead, Columbus reached Cuba and spent Christmas 1492 in Haiti.

This map shows Columbus' route in 1492. The voyage took 32 weeks, and his ships arrived back in Palos on 14th March, 1493.

Columbus carried on exploring in other voyages to Jamaica and parts of South America. Later, Spain became rich from these new lands. Columbus never reached the East, and never believed that he had discovered a whole new continent.

A different route

There was a route to the East across the Indian Ocean, as Bartholemew Diaz had so nearly discovered in 1488.

The Portuguese explorer Vasco da Gama was the first European to reach Asia by this route. His four ships reached in India in May, 1498.

He filled his ship with valuable spices in India, and was rewarded by King Manoel of Portugal when he returned home in 1499.

Around the World

Francis Drake

Francis Drake was born in England in about 1543. He went to sea when he was only a boy and commanded his first ship when he was about 21 years old.

At that time, people thought there was a continent called "Terra Australis Incognita" ("unknown southern land"). They thought it lay to the south of America.

In 1577, Queen Elizabeth I sent Drake to attack Spanish ships carrying treasure from South America. He was also told to look for the unknown land.

The hunt for treasure

In December, 1577, Drake left Plymouth in England in command of five ships and 160 men. His ship was specially named the *Golden Hind* for this voyage.

The *Golden Hind* returned alone to England three years later. Drake had not found an unknown land but he had sailed around the world. He brought back many rich treasures for the Queen.

The cross-staff

Drake used a cross-staff made of two pieces of wood to help him navigate. To use it, he held one end up to his eye, pointing the other towards the sun.

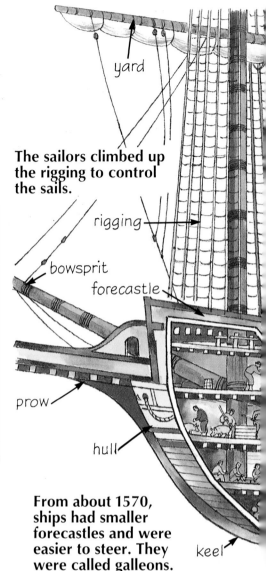

The sailors climbed up the rigging to control the sails.

yard, rigging, bowsprit, forecastle, prow, hull, keel

From about 1570, ships had smaller forecastles and were easier to steer. They were called galleons.

He moved the shorter, sliding part of the cross-staff up and down the longer piece until he could see the sun at one end and the horizon at the other.

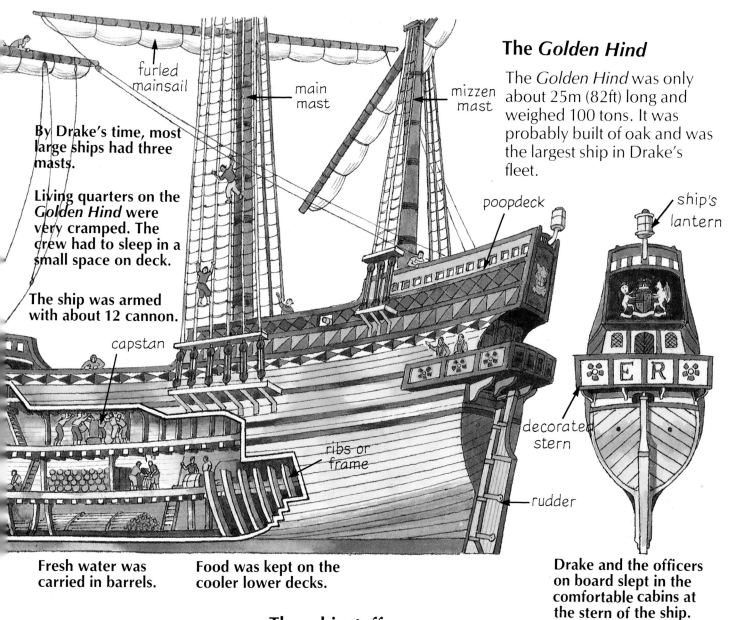

By Drake's time, most large ships had three masts.

furled mainsail

main mast

mizzen mast

Living quarters on the *Golden Hind* were very cramped. The crew had to sleep in a small space on deck.

The ship was armed with about 12 cannon.

capstan

poopdeck

ribs or frame

The *Golden Hind*

The *Golden Hind* was only about 25m (82ft) long and weighed 100 tons. It was probably built of oak and was the largest ship in Drake's fleet.

ship's lantern

decorated stern

rudder

Fresh water was carried in barrels.

Food was kept on the cooler lower decks.

Drake and the officers on board slept in the comfortable cabins at the stern of the ship.

The whipstaff

Ships at that time were steered by a whipstaff attached to the tiller. This lever could change the position of the rudder when swung from side to side.

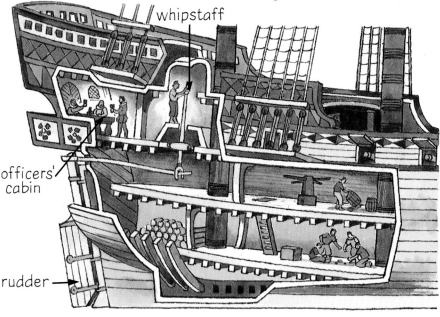

whipstaff

officers' cabin

rudder

The staff had notches on it. He noted which notch the cross-piece had reached. When he looked at his charts, he could now work out the ship's position.

Building a ship

Building a wooden ship was hard work. Timber had to be carefully chosen and shaped by hand with simple hand tools. There were no drawn plans to work from.

Shipbuilding tools

compass saw

chisel

compass with chalk

draw knife

inside calipers

pincers

crow bar

caulking mallet

brace and bit

caulking iron and hammer

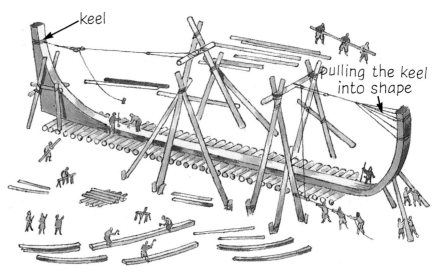

keel

pulling the keel into shape

Shipbuilders began a ship by laying down the keel. This is the strong wooden "backbone" of the ship.

It was cut out of long lengths of hard wood such as oak, and shaped with a tool called an adze.

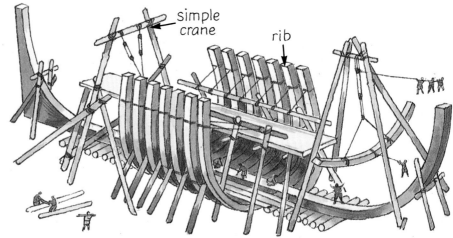

simple crane

rib

Next, the ribs of the ships were added. These were large, curved timbers which were joined to the keel.

Each rib was lifted into position by a simple crane. A large wooden sailing ship had about 25 ribs on each side.

The right wood

Shipbuilders often used oak for the keel and ribs because it is strong. Pine was used for masts because the trees grow tall and straight.

Shipbuilders searched for pieces of wood that were nearly the right shape for each part of the ship. Each one was carefully chosen.

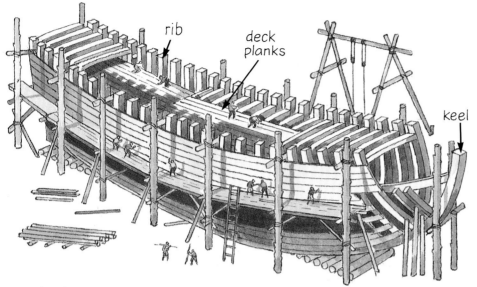

rib

deck planks

keel

English handsaw

auger

chalk line and reel

adzes

maul

Swedish chopping axe

Dutch rule

English broad axe

Planks were then fitted along the ship's sides. Each plank was softened in steam and bent into the right shape.

They were then nailed in place. The decks were added next, with beams across the hull to support them.

poopdeck

hull

prow

The hull had to be made completely watertight. Rope dipped in tar was hammered into the gaps between the

planks. This was called caulking. The ship was then launched and taken to the fitting out berth.

Fitting-out

hold

The inside of the ship was finished at the fitting-out berth. Masts, sails and rigging were added there, as well as cannon if it was a warship.

Its cabins were furnished and a stove put in the brick-lined galley. With supplies on board, the ship was ready for its crew.

Pirates

Ever since ships have carried cargo, pirates have attacked them to steal whatever they found on board, terrifying sailors with their guns and cutlasses.

Pirates were ruthless outlaws who would be put in prison if they went home. Their small, fast ships lay in wait for any large, slow cargo ships far out at sea.

In the 1600s and early 1700s, thousands of ships were carrying valuable cargoes back to Europe. These ships made easy targets for pirates. They attacked ships full of gold from South America and silks and gems from the East.

Attacking a ship

Pirates knew that merchant ships were not heavily armed. The sight of a pirate ship coming alongside was often enough to make such a ship surrender without a fight.

Blackbeard

Edward Teach was a famous British pirate captain. He stuck pieces of burning rope in his long beard in battle to frighten his enemies. He was called Blackbeard, and he died in 1718 in a battle with a naval ship sent to capture him.

Lady pirates

Mary Read and Ann Bonny were women pirates in the crew of John Rackham, Bonny's husband. They were very fierce fighters and robbed many ships. They were captured and killed in Jamaica in 1720.

Pirate ships

Pirates often stole their ships. They were small, fast and armed with large cannon and many smaller guns.

A pirate crew was a mixed bunch of men. Some were criminals who had run away to sea. Others were sailors taken from captured ships and forced into piracy.

When pirates robbed a ship, each member of the crew was given a share of the clothes, jewels and money stolen from the passengers.

Boarding a ship

The pirate ship sailed alongside its victim. The pirates threw grappling hooks on ropes to hold the two ships together. With cannon firing, the pirates climbed on board the captive ship and fought with cutlasses and pistols. If they won, they loaded any treasure on to their ship.

Walking the plank

People think pirates made their prisoners walk the plank. This was rare, as they were useful as crewmen.

Caught!

When pirates were caught by naval ships, they were usually hanged. Their bodies were sometimes hung in a public place as a warning to criminals. The famous pirate Captain Kidd was hung in chains in 1701.

Floating fortresses

During the 18th century, the powerful navies of Europe such as Britain and France, built large, heavily-armed sailing ships to fight at sea.

These were called "men-of-war". The biggest had over 100 cannon on board and a crew of about 900 men.

First-rate

Warships at that time were rated by how many guns they carried. A ship had to carry over 100 guns to be a first-rate ship.

First-rate ships were the biggest, most powerful warships afloat. They were about 61m (200ft) long and 15m (50ft) wide.

Firing a cannon

A first-rate carried cannon of several different sizes. This one fired a cannonball weighing as much as 10kg (24lbs). Up to 15 men formed the crew for each gun, firing every two minutes.

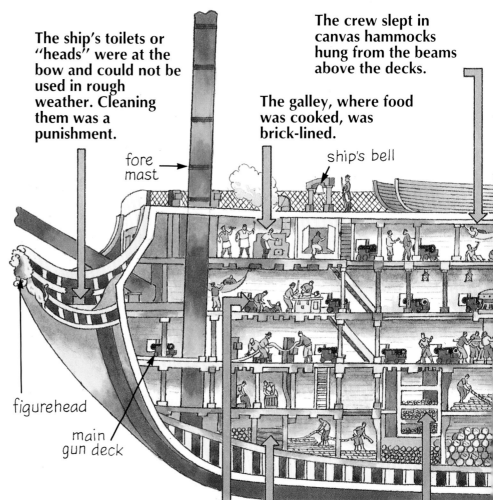

The ship's toilets or "heads" were at the bow and could not be used in rough weather. Cleaning them was a punishment.

The crew slept in canvas hammocks hung from the beams above the decks.

The galley, where food was cooked, was brick-lined.

fore mast

ship's bell

figurehead

main gun deck

When sailors were wounded in battle or fell ill, they were treated in the sick bay by the ship's doctor.

Stores of ropes and sails were kept in the hold. Food was also kept here because it was cooler.

Once a cannon had been fired, it was pulled back. The gun barrel was cleaned and cooled with a wet sponge.

The loaders then pushed a canvas bag of gunpowder down to the end of the barrel with a rammer.

The cannonball was loaded into the front, or muzzle, of the gun. A wad of rope stopped it from rolling out.

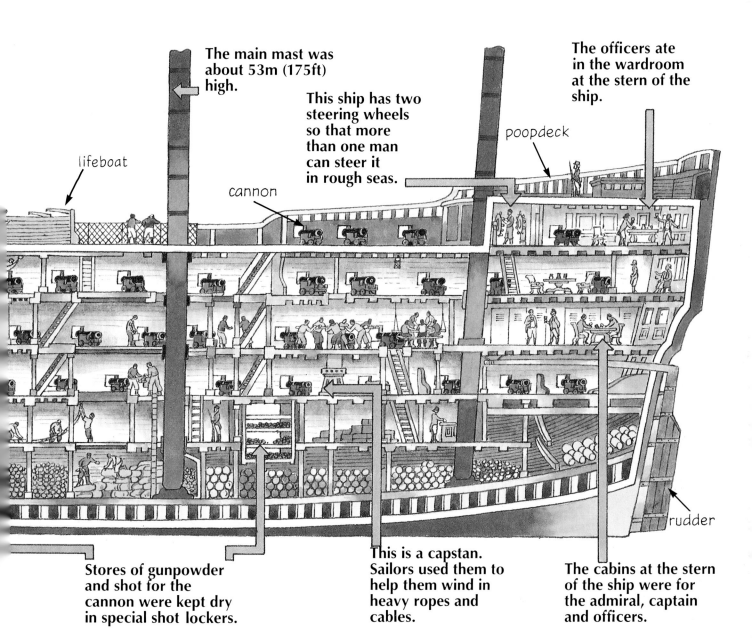

The main mast was about 53m (175ft) high.

The officers ate in the wardroom at the stern of the ship.

This ship has two steering wheels so that more than one man can steer it in rough seas.

poopdeck

lifeboat

cannon

Stores of gunpowder and shot for the cannon were kept dry in special shot lockers.

This is a capstan. Sailors used them to help them wind in heavy ropes and cables.

rudder

The cabins at the stern of the ship were for the admiral, captain and officers.

The gun crew pulled on ropes until the muzzle of the gun was pointing out of the side of the ship. The gunner aimed the cannon.

The gunner filled a small hole at the back of the cannon with gunpowder. He then lit the powder.

The gunpowder then exploded, and shot the cannonball out of the barrel. The gun jumped backwards, but was held by ropes.

Life at sea

Life for sailors in the 1700s and 1800s was harsh. They worked long, hard hours and were punished for any offense. They were poorly paid and their food was often bad. They died of fevers or of horrible wounds in battle.

The press gang

During a war, groups of seamen called press gangs captured able-bodied men and forced them to go to sea.

This cruel way of finding a crew for warships was called impressment. It was stopped in about 1850.

A sailor's day

A sailor's day at that time was divided into six periods of duty called watches. Each one was four hours long and was marked by the ship's bell.

The ship's crew was split into two or three groups. These were also called watches. One watch could rest below decks while the others were on duty.

The sailor's day began when the boatswain blew his whistle. This woke the men on the first watch of the day.

They climbed the masts to unfurl the sails. If a fair wind was blowing, the ship moved on its way.

At about 11.30 am, sailors on British ships were given their daily ration of half-a-pint of rum and water, called grog.

During the day, the sailors cleaned weapons, washed the decks and paintwork and did repair work on the ship.

The men off duty had supper at 5 pm. They carried it down from the galley to the lower decks to eat.

The sailors hung up their hammocks to sleep in at around 8 pm. They were only about 0.3m(1ft) apart.

Sailors' clothes

Sailors did not have uniforms until about 1850, although officers began wearing them in the 1700s.

A captain in the Royal Navy of about 150 years ago wore a long blue tail-coat with brass buttons. He had gold epaulettes on his shoulders and a white shirt.

Ordinary sailors wore baggy trousers called breeches and a loose shirt. They had very few clothes and were given one afternoon each week to mend them.

telescope

epaulettes

Ship's food

Food on board a ship during the 1700s and 1800s was unhealthy. Fresh fruit and vegetables soon rotted.

Sailors often ate only dry ship's biscuit, salted meat and dried fish. Cheese and flour became maggoty.

cheese · ship's biscuit · maggots · salted meat · rat · pickled cabbage · dried fish

Scurvy

Until the 1700s, many thousands of sailors died of a horrible disease called scurvy. People did not know what caused it. In 1753, it was proved that oranges, lemons and limes cured scurvy, and a sailor's diet improved.

Discipline on board

For a punishment, sailors were flogged with a whip called a cat o' nine tails. Although no sailor was supposed to be given more than 12 lashes, some captains were brutal and gave more.

The "Cat"

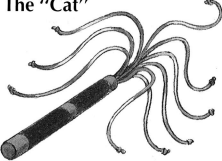

A cat o' nine tails had nine pieces of cord attached to its wooden handle. Each cord had three knots in it. Twelve lashes were enough to cut a man's back. Salt was rubbed into the cuts to heal them.

The first steamships

When the steam engine was first invented in about 1715, people tried to build a ship powered by steam. Such a ship would not have to rely on the wind to move forwards.

Paddle wheels

flat paddle blades

The largest paddle wheels were about 17m (56ft) wide.

The first steam ships had paddle wheels. Paddle wheels had flat blades which dipped into the water, pushing the ship along. They were turned by the ship's steam engine. Each wheel had a wooden guard.

The *Britannia*

By 1800, the first successful steamships were launched. The *Britannia* was a wooden paddle steamer, built in 1840.

spar

lifeboat

stern

How a steam engine works

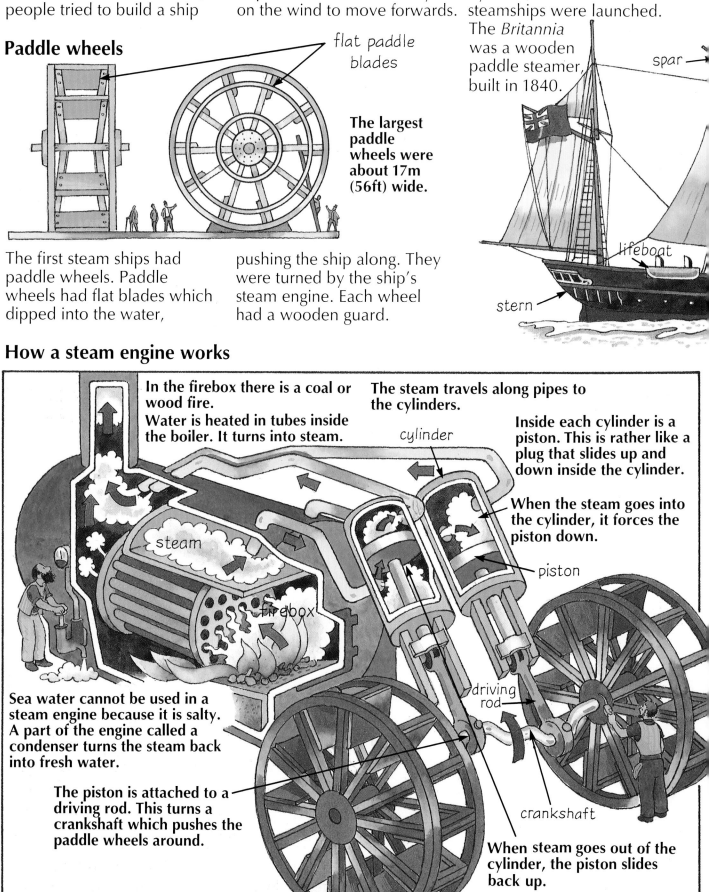

In the firebox there is a coal or wood fire.
Water is heated in tubes inside the boiler. It turns into steam.

The steam travels along pipes to the cylinders.

cylinder

Inside each cylinder is a piston. This is rather like a plug that slides up and down inside the cylinder.

When the steam goes into the cylinder, it forces the piston down.

steam

piston

firebox

Sea water cannot be used in a steam engine because it is salty. A part of the engine called a condenser turns the steam back into fresh water.

driving rod

The piston is attached to a driving rod. This turns a crankshaft which pushes the paddle wheels around.

crankshaft

When steam goes out of the cylinder, the piston slides back up.

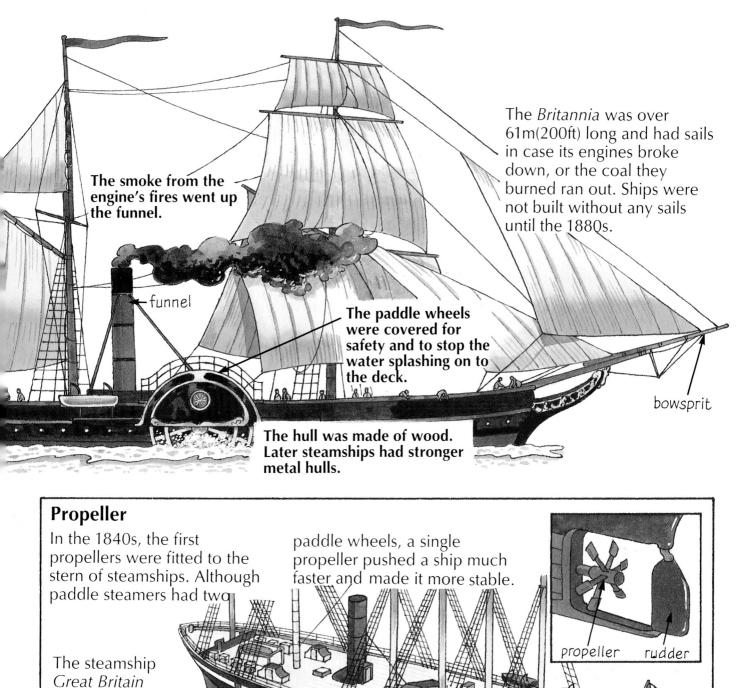

The smoke from the engine's fires went up the funnel.

funnel

The *Britannia* was over 61m(200ft) long and had sails in case its engines broke down, or the coal they burned ran out. Ships were not built without any sails until the 1880s.

The paddle wheels were covered for safety and to stop the water splashing on to the deck.

bowsprit

The hull was made of wood. Later steamships had stronger metal hulls.

Propeller

In the 1840s, the first propellers were fitted to the stern of steamships. Although paddle steamers had two paddle wheels, a single propeller pushed a ship much faster and made it more stable.

The steamship *Great Britain* was designed by the famous British designer I.K. Brunel. It was the first ship with a propeller and an iron hull to cross the Atlantic, in 1843.

propeller   rudder

steam cylinder   propeller shaft   propeller

Tug-of-war

In 1845, a tug-of-war was held to see whether a propeller was more powerful than paddle wheels.

Two boats of about the same size were joined by a cable and steamed at full speed in opposite directions.

The *Rattler*, with the propeller,

Rattler

Alecto

easily pulled the paddle steamer, the *Alecto*, backwards. This tug-of-war proved to shipbuilders of the 19th century that propellers were more powerful than paddles.

29

The last days of sail

The biggest, fastest and most beautiful sailing ships were built in the 19th century. Cargoes were shipped all over the world by sail and shipowners with fleets of merchant ships became very rich. Millions of people left Europe in the 1800s. They went to start new lives thousands of miles away in America, Australia and New Zealand.

Emigration by sail

Between 1819 and 1859, more than five million people emigrated from Europe.

They went hoping to make a better life for themselves in the new lands.

Wealthy passengers travelled in comfort. They relaxed in lounges during the long weeks of the voyage.

Poorer passengers slept in a space only 2m(6ft) long and 1m(3ft) wide. There were few toilets and no bathrooms.

Emigrants had to bring their own food and cook it on deck. In bad weather, they were locked below.

Botany Bay

Between 1787 and 1840, the British government sent 74,000 criminals to Australia because the jails were full.

In January 1788, a fleet of 11 sailing ships arrived in Botany Bay, after eight months at sea. The 700 convicts on board became Australia's first settlers.

Sailing speed

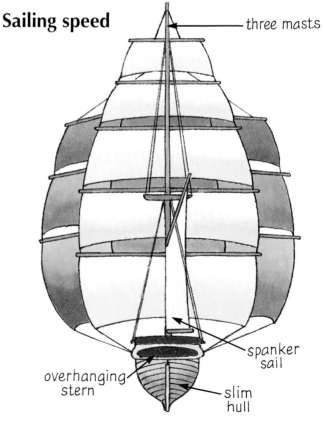

three masts

spanker sail

overhanging stern

slim hull

Ships were now fitted with more sails. Their hulls were made longer and sleeker to cut through water more quickly.

Clippers

The fastest cargo sailing ships were clippers. They carried cargoes which had to be delivered quickly.

In 1848, clippers offered the fastest passage to California when gold was discovered there. A gold rush started.

The skilful clipper captains wanted to break speed records and they raced against each other.

The tea race

The first cargo of the new tea crop in China could be sold for a high price. Clippers raced to deliver it.

crates of tea

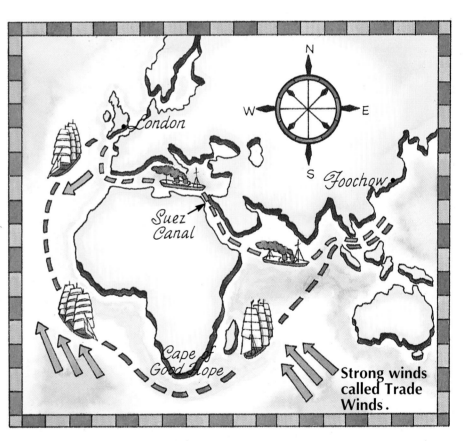

Strong winds called Trade Winds.

A famous tea race took place in 1866. On 30th May, 1866 the clippers *Ariel* and *Taeping* left Foochow in China on the 25,600km (16,000 mile) trip to London.

Both clipper captains were excellent seamen. After 99 days at sea, the *Taeping* sailed up the River Thames on 6th September only half-an-hour ahead of the *Ariel*.

By the middle of the 19th century, steamships had taken over many of the profitable cargo routes from the clippers. Steamships did not have to rely on the wind.

In 1869, the Suez Canal was opened. Clippers could not pass through it because there was not enough wind. Steamships could now beat any sailing ship carrying cargo.

The Ironclads

From the 1820s onwards, warships were fitted with bigger, more powerful guns. By 1880, they no longer fired cannonballs but bullet-shaped pieces of metal called shells.

Wooden ships were not strong enough to stand up to these guns. Ships were protected with iron plates, and were called ironclads.

Clash of the Ironclads

Merrimac

Monitor

iron plating

armored turret

Two of the first ironclads were used in the American Civil War (1861-1865). The *Monitor* had iron plating 25cm(10in) thick, and two guns inside an armored turret.

The *Merrimac* had iron plates 10cm(4in) thick, and six guns. When they met in battle in 1862, neither ship won because their round shells bounced off the iron plates.

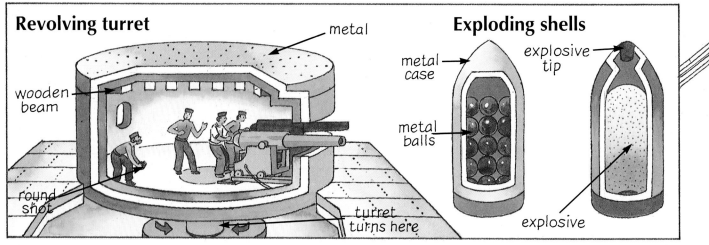

Revolving turret

metal

wooden beam

round shot

turret turns here

Exploding shells

metal case

metal balls

explosive tip

explosive

The *Monitor*'s revolving gun turret was 6m(19ft) wide and 3m(9ft) high. Its guns could fire shells in any direction.

The *Merrimac*'s guns fired shells which exploded when they hit an object. They were shaped to pierce metal hulls.

Some shells showered small pieces of metal, called shrapnel, when they exploded.

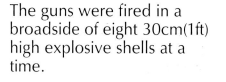

anchor

main gun turret

The *Dreadnought*

In February 1906, the *Dreadnought* was launched in Portsmouth, Britain. It had 24 big guns and weighed 17,900 tons.

The *Dreadnought*'s guns were arranged in five turrets. They could be loaded, aimed and fired in 30 seconds.

The guns were fired in a broadside of eight 30cm(1ft) high explosive shells at a time.

It carried a crew of 727 officers and men. Wireless was used to help the battleship navigate.

The *Devastation*

The *Devastation* was built in Britain in 1872 and had no sails or rigging to get in the way of gunfire.

It was driven by a steam engine and could carry 1,800 tons of coal. Its four guns weighed 35 tons each, and were in two revolving turrets.

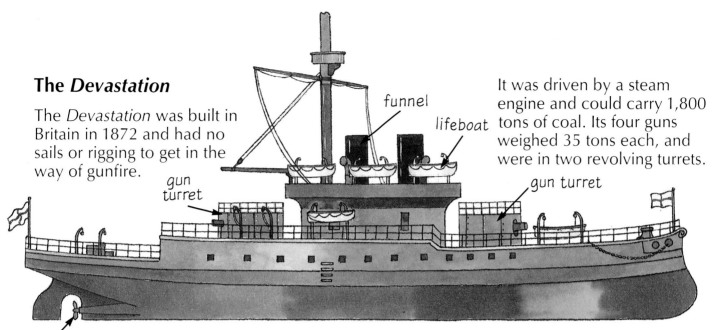

funnel

lifeboat

gun turret

gun turret

propeller

Breech loading guns

breech   muzzle

By the 1880s, guns on warships were loaded from the back (breech) rather than from the front (muzzle). This made firing a gun quicker.

The cartridge was placed behind the shell and both were shut in by a strong door. The cartridge was set off and everyone stood clear.

The *Dreadnought* had very powerful engines and could travel faster than any other ship at that time.

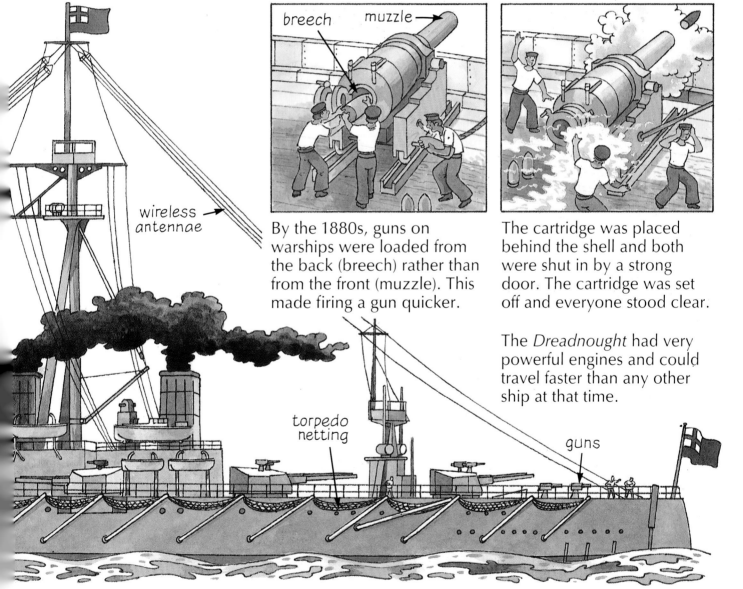

wireless antennae

torpedo netting

guns

The bow had steel armor 15cm(6in) thick, the stern had a layer nearly 10cm(4in) thick.

The *Dreadnought* was over 152m(500ft) long and 24m(80ft) wide.

The battleship had more than twice the gunpower of any other battleship of its time.

Ocean liners

At the end of the 19th century, large, comfortable passenger ships called ocean liners were built. The most famous belonged to the Cunard Line.

Liners were much faster than earlier steamships. In the 1870s, it took about nine days to cross the Atlantic. In 1909, the *R.M.S. Mauretania* crossed in only four days.

The *Mauretania*

The Cunard shipping company launched the *R.M.S. Mauretania* in 1907. It was the biggest liner ever built and could carry 2,165 first, second and third class passengers.

With its four screw propellers it held the Blue Riband between 1909 to 1929.

funnel

promenade

lifeboat

These are some of the provisions carried on a liner of about 1900.

6,000 chickens

17,000 dozen eggs

1,000 blocks of ice cream

Ocean liners were like floating cities. They had hundreds of different rooms including shops, hairdressers and a post office for their passengers.

Life on board

Meals had six courses in the first-class dining room. Fresh bread was baked on board in the ship's bakery.

Dances were sometimes held in the evenings. The ship's orchestra played as the passengers danced.

The passengers could stroll along the ship's promenade, play games on deck or read books from the library.

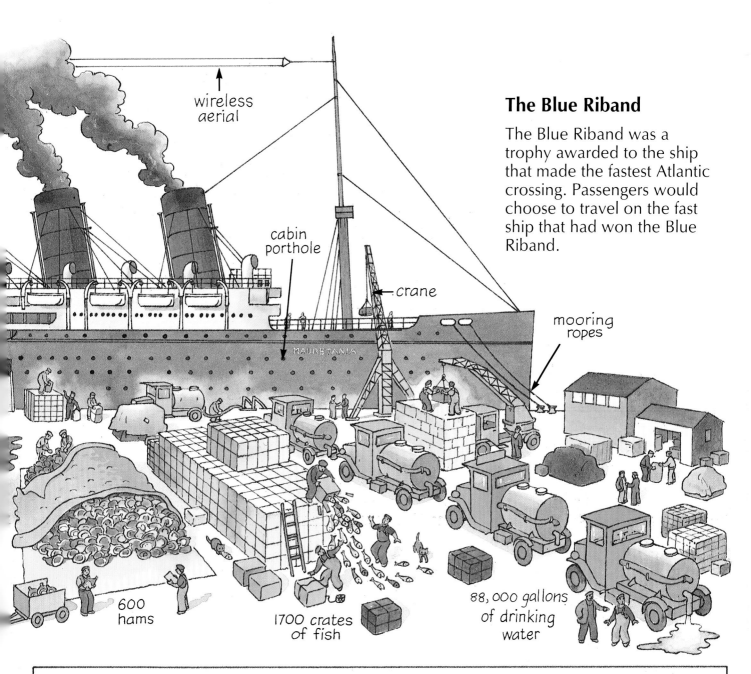

wireless
aerial

cabin
porthole

crane

MAURETANIA

mooring
ropes

600
hams

1700 crates
of fish

88,000 gallons
of drinking
water

The Blue Riband

The Blue Riband was a trophy awarded to the ship that made the fastest Atlantic crossing. Passengers would choose to travel on the fast ship that had won the Blue Riband.

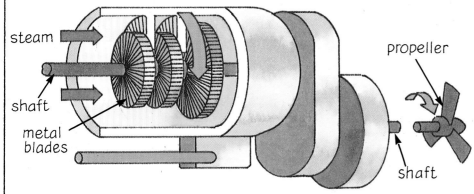

Steam turbines

In 1894, a British engineer, Charles Parsons, invented the turbine engine.

It drove ships faster by using jets of steam from the ship's boilers.

steam

shaft

metal
blades

propeller

shaft

How they work

The steam hits metal blades attached to a shaft. The shaft is joined to the ship's propeller. When the blades spin, this turns the propeller.

The *Turbinia*

TURBINIA

The first turbine engine was fitted to the *Turbinia* in 1897. It was so successful that turbine engines were soon fitted to both battleships and liners.

Submarines

People tried for over 400 years to build ships that could move underwater. An underwater ship would be invisible and would be able to make surprise attacks on other ships.

Submarines must be able to dive and surface easily and to move under the water. Their crews must also have a supply of air to breathe.

Early submarines

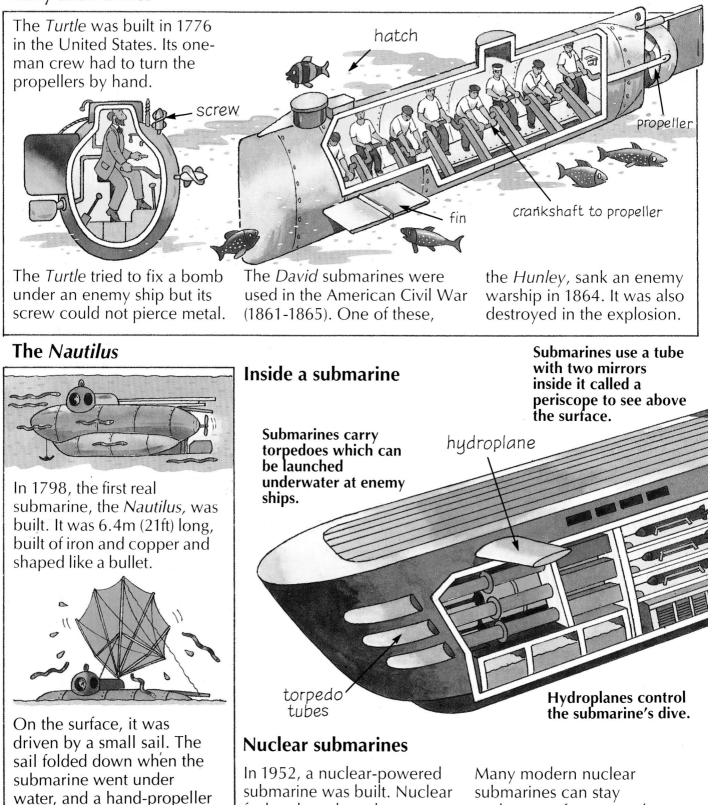

The *Turtle* was built in 1776 in the United States. Its one-man crew had to turn the propellers by hand.

hatch

screw

propeller

crankshaft to propeller

fin

The *Turtle* tried to fix a bomb under an enemy ship but its screw could not pierce metal.

The *David* submarines were used in the American Civil War (1861-1865). One of these,

the *Hunley*, sank an enemy warship in 1864. It was also destroyed in the explosion.

The *Nautilus*

In 1798, the first real submarine, the *Nautilus,* was built. It was 6.4m (21ft) long, built of iron and copper and shaped like a bullet.

On the surface, it was driven by a small sail. The sail folded down when the submarine went under water, and a hand-propeller was used.

Inside a submarine

Submarines carry torpedoes which can be launched underwater at enemy ships.

Submarines use a tube with two mirrors inside it called a periscope to see above the surface.

hydroplane

torpedo tubes

Hydroplanes control the submarine's dive.

Nuclear submarines

In 1952, a nuclear-powered submarine was built. Nuclear fuel on board produces power to drive the turbines.

Many modern nuclear submarines can stay underwater for two to three years without refuelling.

The Submarine

In 1944, submarines were fitted with a breathing tube, called a schnorkel. The crew could breathe when they were 9m(30ft) under the water. By the 1950s, submarines had machines to clean the air for the crew during long dives.

Submarines were fitted with steam-powered turbine engines at this time, and could stay underwater for much longer.

Diving

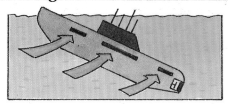

A submarine has large ballast tanks which fill with water when valves are opened. The submarine then dives.

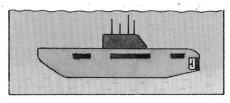

When it has reached the right depth, the valves are closed. The submarine will stay at this depth.

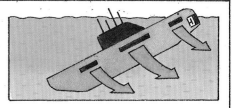

For the submarine to surface, air, forced into the tanks, pushes the water out as it floats up.

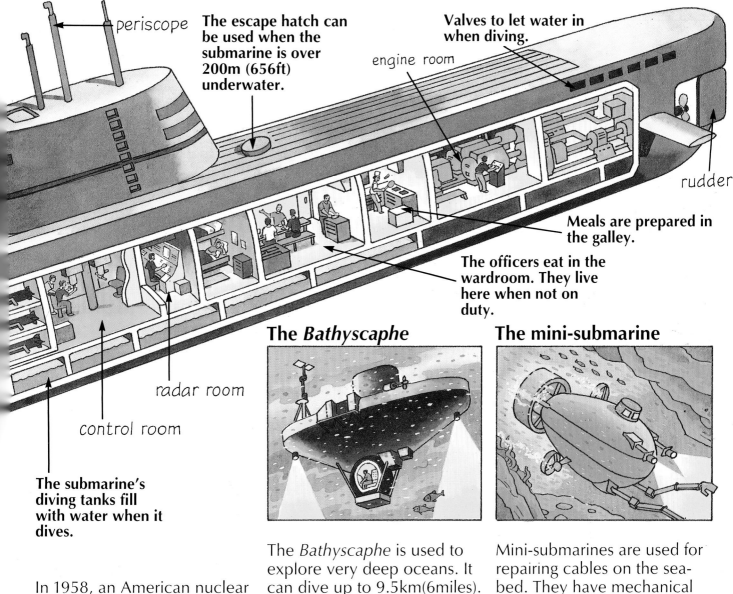

periscope

The escape hatch can be used when the submarine is over 200m (656ft) underwater.

Valves to let water in when diving.

engine room

rudder

Meals are prepared in the galley.

The officers eat in the wardroom. They live here when not on duty.

radar room

control room

The submarine's diving tanks fill with water when it dives.

In 1958, an American nuclear submarine called the *Nautilus* travelled under the Arctic ice to the North Pole.

The *Bathyscaphe*

The *Bathyscaphe* is used to explore very deep oceans. It can dive up to 9.5km(6miles). Its hull is very thick so that it is not crushed by the water pressure.

The mini-submarine

Mini-submarines are used for repairing cables on the sea-bed. They have mechanical arms that can pick things up. Some are controlled by computer and a robot.

37

Cargo ships

Ships carry cargo all over the world. Some are built specially for certain cargoes and the biggest cargo ships carry oil from the Middle East to Europe. They are called tankers and the oil is stored in tanks inside the hull.

Building a big ship

Since the Second World War (1939-1945), large cargo ships have been built in parts which are then put together.

Ship workers make sections of the ship in the right order in sheds arranged around the building berth.

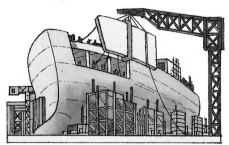

The parts are lifted into position by crane and welded together to make the hull. The ship is then fitted out.

Offshore oil terminal

Some very large tankers, called supertankers, are too big to fit into a harbor. They pump their cargo of oil into tanks several miles offshore.

Helicopter coming in to land on tanker helipad.

Oil terminal

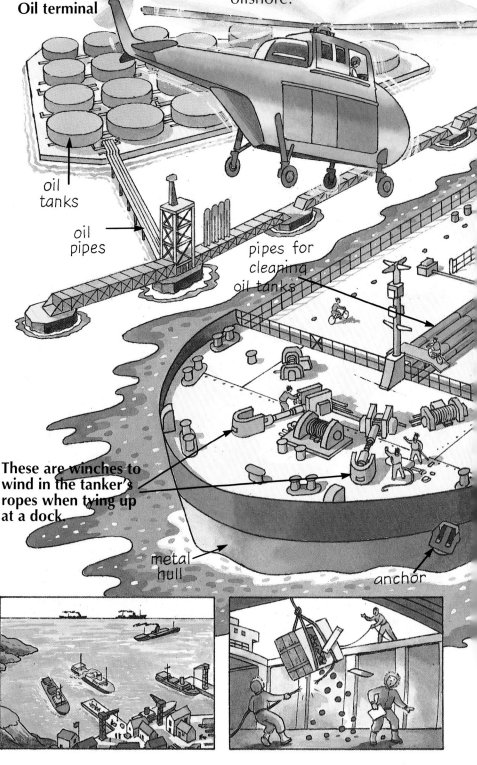

oil tanks

oil pipes

pipes for cleaning oil tanks

These are winches to wind in the tanker's ropes when tying up at a dock.

metal hull

anchor

Other cargo ships

The first ship with tanks for its cargo was the *Glückauf*, built in 1886. It had sails as well as a steam engine.

In the early 1900s, steamers went between ports carrying many different cargoes. They were called "tramps".

Some ships carry cargoes of food, such as fruit and meat. Their holds are refrigerated to keep them cold.

Life on board

The crew of an oil tanker are at sea for weeks. They can go to the movies on board, swim in the swimming pool, or play games in the crew lounge.

This crane lifts the heavy oil pipes on board the tanker.

radar mast

funnel

control deck

life boat

helipad

observation point

spare propeller

Radar

Radar was first used to show the position of enemy ships and submarines in the Second World War.

radar disc

How it works

The ship sends out soundless radio waves in all directions.

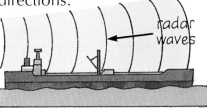

radar waves

When the waves hit another object, they bounce back.

The ship's radar screen shows the position of other ships or airplanes in the area.

Oil tankers

This tanker carries enough oil in its tanks to fill 17,000 fuel trucks.

Some tankers are so large that the crew ride bikes to move about on deck.

Container ships

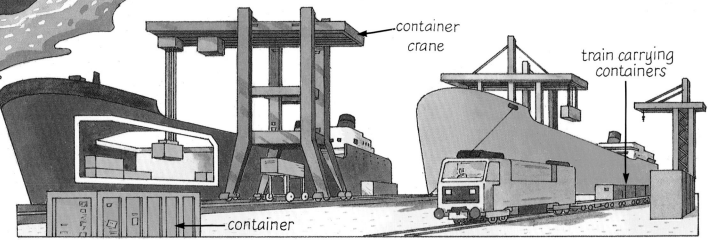

container crane

train carrying containers

container

Cargo is packed in metal containers about 12m(40ft) long and 2.5m(8ft) wide.

The containers are loaded on board ship by cranes which slide along the dock on rails.

Containers can be lifted straight on to trains or trucks without being unpacked.

Hovercraft and hydrofoils

A ship could move much faster if it did not have to push through water. The less a ship touches the water, the faster it can go.

Today's fastest passenger ships, hovercraft and hydrofoils, skim over the water.

Hovercraft

Hovercraft are also called air-cushion vehicles or ACVs. Their hulls do not touch the water because they are held up by a cushion of air. They can go much faster than ordinary boats and can skim over 1.5m(5ft) waves.

The first hovercraft was built and tested in 1958 by Sir Christopher Cockrell, a British engineer. Hovercraft can now carry over 250 passengers and 30 cars across the English Channel in 35 minutes. Ferries take 1½ hours on the shortest route.

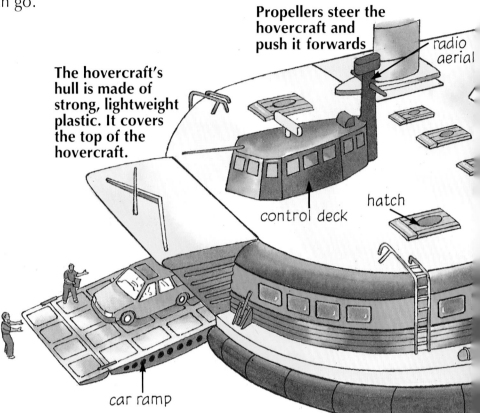

Propellers steer the hovercraft and push it forwards

radio aerial

The hovercraft's hull is made of strong, lightweight plastic. It covers the top of the hovercraft.

control deck

hatch

car ramp

Hovercraft on land

Hovercraft do not tie up in a harbor like boats. They glide up a ramp on to dry land.

When the fans are switched off, the hovercraft gently settles down.

The hovercraft's air cushion makes travelling over choppy water or bumpy ground much smoother.

Expedition

Hovercraft can move quickly over rough, wet ground. An expedition used them in the swamps of the Amazon.

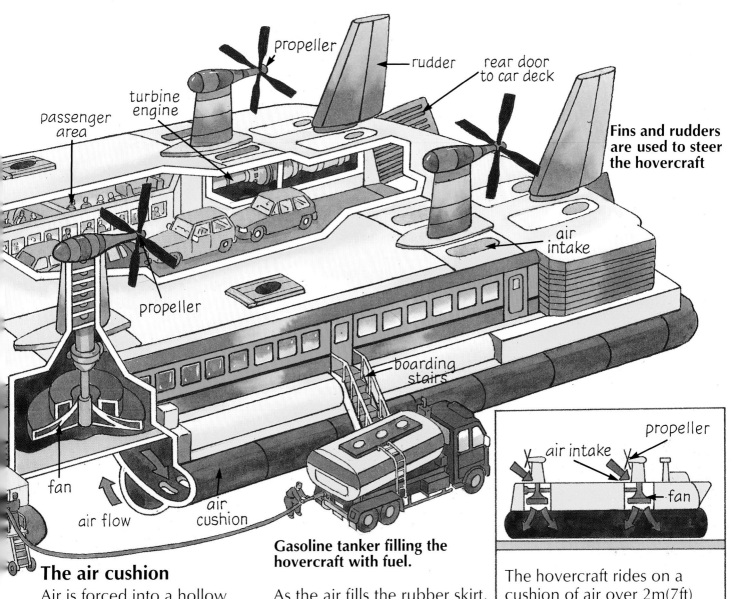

passenger
area

turbine
engine

propeller

rudder

rear door
to car deck

**Fins and rudders
are used to steer
the hovercraft**

air
intake

propeller

boarding
stairs

fan

air flow

air
cushion

**Gasoline tanker filling the
hovercraft with fuel.**

air intake

propeller

fan

The air cushion

Air is forced into a hollow
chamber inside the hovercraft
by powerful fans.

As the air fills the rubber skirt,
it lifts the hovercraft off the
ground.

The hovercraft rides on a
cushion of air over 2m(7ft)
high. The thick rubbery skirt
keeps the air in.

Hydrofoils

Hydrofoils are ships that speed through the
water on underwater "wings" called foils.
The foils slice easily through the water and a
hydrofoil can go very fast.

The first hydrofoil was built in 1906. It
reached a speed of 66.7 kmph(41mph).
Hydrofoils do not go faster than 90kmph
(56mph) in case they break up.

How they work

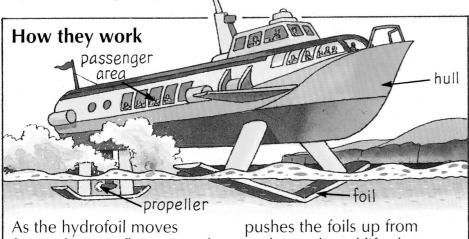

passenger
area

hull

propeller

foil

As the hydrofoil moves
forward, water flows over the
surface of the foils. Water

pushes the foils up from
underneath and lifts the
hydrofoil out of the water.

Some foils look like legs when
the ship is skimming over the
water. These are more
suitable for choppy water.
Others have v-shaped wings.

Boats for pleasure

Boats are no longer used just for carrying cargo or fare-paying passengers.

People all over the world now sail in boats for pleasure.

Pleasure yacht

This yacht is suitable for a family sailing holiday.

It is safe to sail on the open sea, and has an engine for days with no wind.

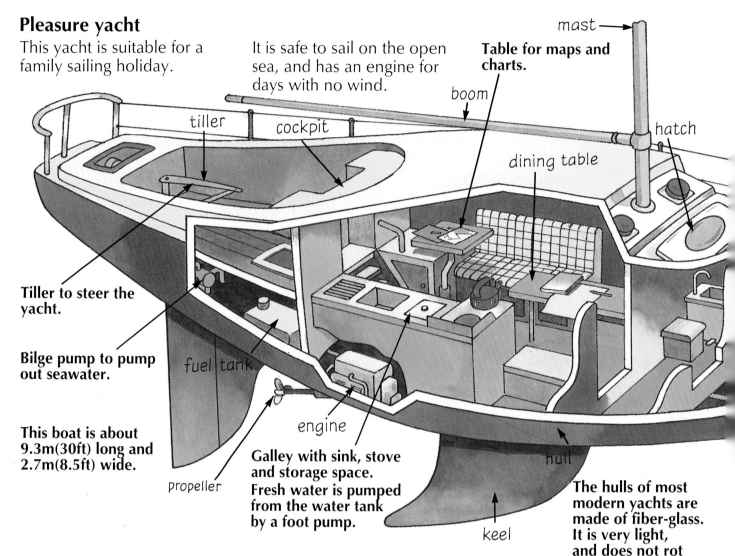

mast

Table for maps and charts.

boom

tiller

cockpit

hatch

dining table

Tiller to steer the yacht.

Bilge pump to pump out seawater.

fuel tank

This boat is about 9.3m(30ft) long and 2.7m(8.5ft) wide.

propeller

engine

Galley with sink, stove and storage space. Fresh water is pumped from the water tank by a foot pump.

hull

keel

The hulls of most modern yachts are made of fiber-glass. It is very light, and does not rot or rust.

Other pleasure boats

Motor cruisers are used for cruising holidays. Some are ocean-going and have large engines.

Kayaks made of fiber-glass can be paddled or raced over rough water on marked courses.

Power boats are built for racing. Some have aircraft engines and have broken world speed records.

Sails

A yacht's sails are arranged in a rig. This is a Bermuda rig, the most common one today.

large triangular mainsail

jib

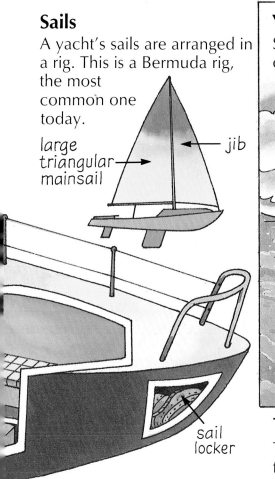

sail locker

Yacht racing

Some yacht races are held on courses near the shore.

Larger yachts race across oceans.

The sails of modern yachts are usually made of man-made material such as nylon.

Single-handed race

Every fourth year since 1960, yachtsmen have raced alone across the Atlantic from Europe to America.

navigation instruments

The voyage takes over 20 days. The yachtsmen keep in radio contact with the shore.

The America's Cup

The America's Cup is a famous yacht race. It was first won by the schooner *America* of the New York Yacht Club in 1851.

This Cup is awarded to the yacht that has beaten its challenger in seven races.

America's Cup.

gaff

tapes to tie up sails

The *America* beat 15 British yachts around the Isle of Wight. The United States held the Cup every year until 1974.

Time Line

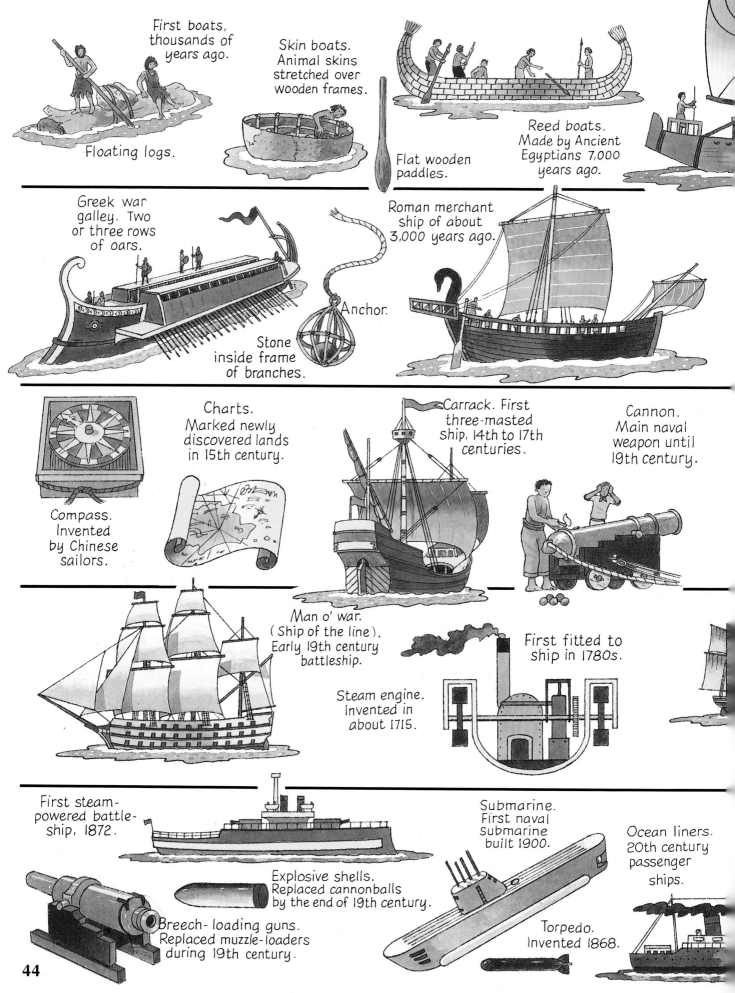

First boats, thousands of years ago.

Floating logs.

Skin boats. Animal skins stretched over wooden frames.

Flat wooden paddles.

Reed boats. Made by Ancient Egyptians 7,000 years ago.

Greek war galley. Two or three rows of oars.

Anchor.

Stone inside frame of branches.

Roman merchant ship of about 3,000 years ago.

Compass. Invented by Chinese sailors.

Charts. Marked newly discovered lands in 15th century.

Carrack. First three-masted ship, 14th to 17th centuries.

Cannon. Main naval weapon until 19th century.

Man o' war. (Ship of the line). Early 19th century battleship.

Steam engine. Invented in about 1715.

First fitted to ship in 1780s.

First steam-powered battle-ship, 1872.

Breech-loading guns. Replaced muzzle-loaders during 19th century.

Explosive shells. Replaced cannonballs by the end of 19th century.

Submarine. First naval submarine built 1900.

Torpedo. Invented 1868.

Ocean liners. 20th century passenger ships.

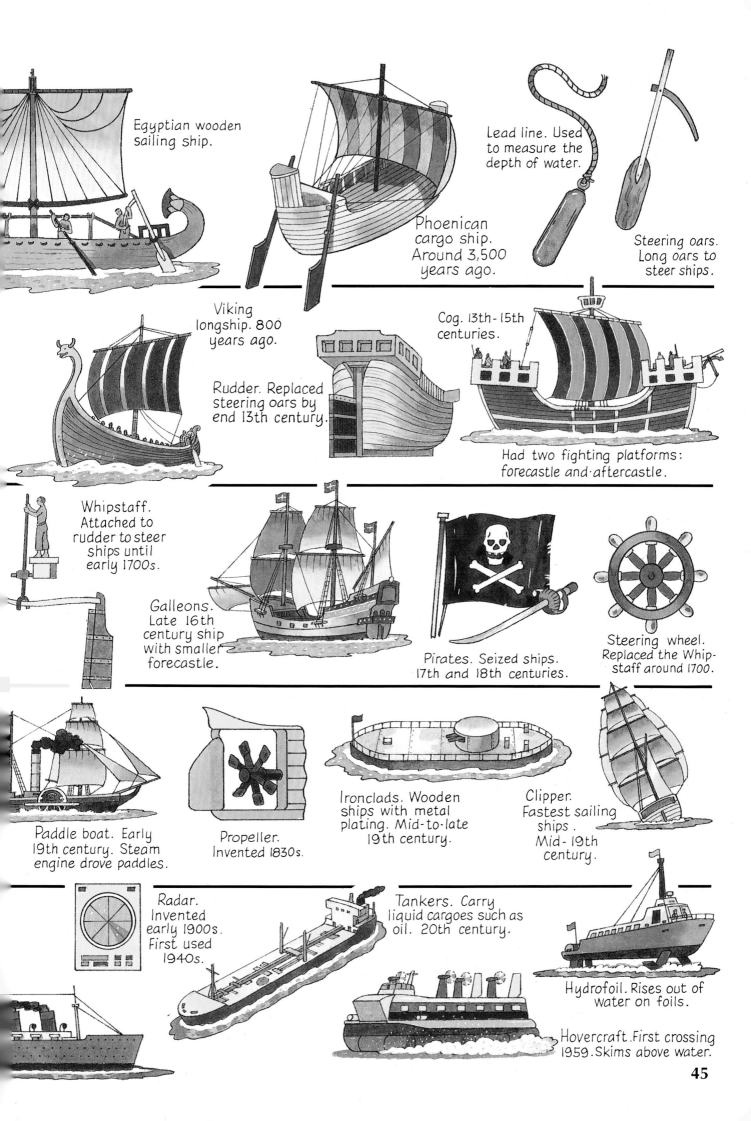

Egyptian wooden sailing ship.

Phoenican cargo ship. Around 3,500 years ago.

Lead line. Used to measure the depth of water.

Steering oars. Long oars to steer ships.

Viking longship. 800 years ago.

Rudder. Replaced steering oars by end 13th century.

Cog. 13th-15th centuries.

Had two fighting platforms: forecastle and aftercastle.

Whipstaff. Attached to rudder to steer ships until early 1700s.

Galleons. Late 16th century ship with smaller forecastle.

Pirates. Seized ships. 17th and 18th centuries.

Steering wheel. Replaced the Whipstaff around 1700.

Paddle boat. Early 19th century. Steam engine drove paddles.

Propeller. Invented 1830s.

Ironclads. Wooden ships with metal plating. Mid-to-late 19th century.

Clipper. Fastest sailing ships. Mid-19th century.

Radar. Invented early 1900s. First used 1940s.

Tankers. Carry liquid cargoes such as oil. 20th century.

Hydrofoil. Rises out of water on foils.

Hovercraft. First crossing 1959. Skims above water.

45

Glossary

Aft: the area towards the rear of ship.

Aftercastle: fighting platform at rear of Medieval ships.

Anchor: heavy weight on rope or chain. Stops ship drifting.

Ballast: weights in bottom of ship to balance it. Can be stone or metal, or cargo.

Berth: 1) place to sleep on a ship. 2) space where ships tie up in harbor.

Biscuit: hard, dry ship's biscuit eaten by sailors until 19th century.

Boom: wooden pole along bottom of sail.

Bow: front end of ship.

Bowsprit: large pole at bow of some ships.

Bridge: raised platform on deck used for steering and navigation.

Broadside: all guns on one side of a ship firing at once.

Bulwark: top part of hull around side of ship.

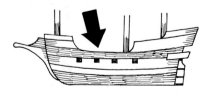

Buoy: floating marker fixed to seabed. Guides ships through channels and marks dangers.

Capsize: when a ship overturns or 'keels over'.

Capstan: machine used to haul up heavy loads, including anchor.

Caulking: plugging the gaps between planks on hulls of wooden ships with tarred rope to make waterproof.

Centerboard: board on sailing dinghies, can be raised or lowered.

Clinker-built: wooden ships built with overlapping planks.

Compass: used to help ships navigate by showing directions.

Cross-staff: wooden instrument used to find latitude in navigation from 13th to 15th centuries.

Deck: the 'floor' of a ship.

Draught: amount of a ship below the water line. See **Plimsoll Line**.

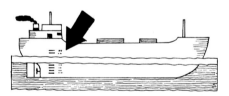

Dry-dock: berth where ship is repaired. Emptied of water.

Even keel: a ship is 'on an even keel' when it is upright in the water and not leaning to either side.

Fathom: distance of 1.8m(6ft). Used to measure depth of water.

Figurehead: carved wooden figure on front of ship.

Fitting-out: adding the insides to a ship once the hull is built.

Foil: shaped 'wing' underneath hydrofoils.

Fore: part towards the front of ship.

Forecastle: fighting platform built at front of ship on Medieval ships.

Gaff: pole along top of mainsail joined to the mast.

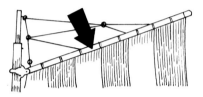

Galley: kitchen area of a ship. (Also a type of rowed ship).

Gangway: ladder or walkway put up to let crew and passengers on and off a ship in harbor.

Grog: mixture of water and rum given to sailors until 19th century.

Gunwale: upper edge of small ship's hull above the waterline.

Hammock: hanging sailor's bed made of rope or canvas.

Harbor: place where ships can tie up at docks. Usually sheltered from strong winds.

Hatch: small door leading to deck above, closed when sailing.

Heads: ship's toilets. At bow of ship.

Helmsman: man who steers the ship.

Hold: where provisions and cargo are stored on board a ship. Sometimes split into several compartments.

Hull: the main part of a ship, its shell.

Hydroplanes: rudders at front and back of submarine to angle diving.

Jib: triangular sail rigged in front of the mast.

Keel: bottom part of hull. Is strong and heavy to help balance the ship.

Lead line: weight on the end of a rope used to measure the depth of water.

Log: captain's diary of voyage.

Magnetic pole: point on the Earth's surface which the needle of a magnetic compass points to. Near the North Pole.

Mainsail: the largest sail of a sailing ship.

Mast: central pole to which sails are attached.

Merchant ship: ship carrying cargo.

Mizzen mast: The furthest mast back on a sailing ship.

Nautical mile: distance of 6,080ft (1,852m) at sea. A land mile is 5,280ft.

Navigate: to work out which way to go.

Paddle wheel: wheel with flat blades on paddle steamers.

Periscope: tube with mirrors used on submarines to see above the surface.

Plimsoll Line: mark on side of ship. Ships must not float lower in the water than this mark when loaded.

Poopdeck: raised deck above officers' cabins at rear of ship.

Port: left side of ship, when facing forwards.

Press gang: group of men who forced men to join the British navy.

Pump: empties the ship of water. Usually placed either side of keel in the bottom of ship.

Rig: sail-plan of a ship.

Rigging: ropes holding masts and sails in position.

Rowlock: U-shaped slot, or leather, wooden or metal loop, which acts as a pivot for the rower to pull the oar against.

Rudder: used to steer ships from the 14th century onwards.

Sextant: instrument used in navigation to find a ship's position.

Spar: wooden or metal pole such as mast, yard or boom, from which sails are hung.

Spinnaker: large, very light triangular sail rigged at front of modern yachts for racing.

Splice: joining two ropes by weaving strands together.

Starboard: the right side of a ship, when facing forwards.

Steering oar: oar at back of ship used for steering until 14th century.

Stern: back end of ship.

Swing a cat (no room to): now used to mean a very small space. From cat o' nine tails whip used to punish sailors.

Tacking: sailing a zigzag course into the wind.

Telescope: tube with lens at both ends. Used to look for and study distant objects.

Tide: rise and fall of the seas, which are attracted by the sun and moon. Changes every 6 hours 20 minutes.

Tiller: the handle which controls the rudder in small ships.

Timbers: ribs or frame of a ship. Large curved pieces of wood that strengthen the hull.

Wake: waves a ship leaves behind it in the water. The wake of large ships can overturn a small boat.

Whipstaff: a lever used to move the rudder in 16th and 17th century ships.

Yard: pole across top of mast from which sail is hung.

Index